POEMS FROM THE SOUTHERN OCEAN

On the ragged edge of the world I'll roam
And the home of the whale shall be my home
And saving seals on the remote ice and snows
The end of my voyage… who knows, who knows?

I have no concerns for the media spins
At the lies and false-hoods they scatter.
May the future forgive my ecological sins
For all other sins don't matter

By
Captain Paul Watson

Poems from The Great Southern Ocean

For over a decade I led annual campaigns to the Southern Ocean Whale Sanctuary to defend endangered and protected Antarctic whales from the illegal whaling activities of the Japanese whaling fleet.

From December through March ever year my ships, officers and crew intervened to stop the slaughter of the whales. We saved more whales than they slew and we have sank the Japanese whaling fleet economically.

In 2019, the Japanese whaling fleet left the Southern Ocean Whale Sanctuary permanently. Our long struggle to stop their illegal operations was successful and we saved the lives of over 6,500 whales.

It was a long and dangerous odyssey, a confrontation between two very stubborn and relentless opponents, between those determined to kill the whales and those of us determined to save their lives.

This book is a collection of some of the campaign poems that have written while in the Southern Ocean onboard the vessels *Farley Mowat*, *Robert Hunter*, *Steve Irwin*, *Bob Barker*, *Gojira*, *Brigitte Bardot*, *Sam Simon* and *Ocean Warrior*.

Campaigns

Operation Minke – 2005 -2006
Operation Leviathan -2006 -2007
Operation Migaloo – 2007 - 2008
Operation Miyamoto Musashi -2008-2009
Operation Matilda – 2009 - 2010
Operation No Compromise – 2010 -2011
Operation Divine Wind – 2011 - 2012
Operation Zero Tolerance – 2012-2013
Operation Relentless – 2013 – 2014
Operation Nemesis – 2016 - 2017

Contents

Son of the Sea
The Death of a Whale
Ask Not for Whom the Whales Bleed. They Bleed for Thee
Knights of Poseidon
Odyssey for the Whales
Trials of a Whale Warrior
The Curse of Ahab's Children
Destroying the Cetacean Death Star
Fighting Whalers in the Great Southern Ocean
Guarding the Southern Gates
My Crew Envisioned in the Eye of My Whale
Snow
The Curse of Ahab's Children
The Death of a Whaler
The Endless Quest
The Sea Shepherd Crew
The Tempest
Whispering Southern Winds
Twilight and Rebirth in the Great Southern Ocean
Verses afloat Upon the Southern Ocean
Whale Wars
Free Me from the Sea
The Happy Exile
Deceitful Betrayal
Sparrow on the Deck
Nowhere Bound
Coming Full Circle
Operation Minke
Operation Leviathan
Operation Migaloo
Operation Miyamoto Musasho
Operation Waltzing Matilda
Operation No Compromise

Operation Divine Wind
Operation Zero Tolerance

Son of the Sea

Swimming alone beneath the darkening sky
Parting water, black as liquid coal
Feeling the deepness, comforted by the swell
The ocean breathing as the waves sigh,
Surf crashing upon a distant shoal
The thunder captured by the Conch's bugled shell.

The Ocean spat the child back onto land,
Spared my life and erased all my fear
I was a child of the wind and of the tide,
At home upon the waves or on sand,
The sea absorbed all my fears and tears
In her loving arms I could securely abide.

Close to a young death I glimpsed an open door,
Birthing awareness within my soul
I understood the sea would not do me wrong.
My Achilles heel does lie ashore,
Nothing to fear from beyond the shoal,
From the deep I heard the siren's haunting song.

A song heard by the ones swallowed by the sea,
Few have heard and walked again on land,
A Siren's voice heard by seals, turtles, and whales.
Imprisoned in my heart, never free,
Rare notes of salt spray, surf, shore and sand,
A song of salvation and a thousand tales.

Magic drapes around me like a wet warm cloak,
Fair passage is mine to come and go,
Beneath, above, and upon the raging flood.
On the crest of the sea fate does float,
Prisoner to wind and tidal floe,
The moon controlling the movement of my blood.

The aquatic spirit of Nemo defines and shapes,
His anger spins the blood in my veins
Ahab's fiery passion haunting my dreams
Freed from the curse of the aquatic apes,
Seizing the issues with controversial reins,
Developing tactics, strategies and schemes.

The ancient mariner did stoppeth me one day,
Standing on the pier, peering deep into his eyes so icy blue,
Seeing truth as naked as a mermaid's form,
As he pointed to the sea to show me the way,
You need a ship he said and you need a crew
For upon the horizon is a gathering storm

Upon the decks of merchants, I did toil,
Reading the ways of the one great ocean,
Crossing and re-crossing her vast expanse
Challenging the wrath of the serpent's coil.
Emotions flowing with the seas changing motion,
Learning her songs and her endless dance.

My calling came with the call from a whale,
Riding upon an Orca's back,
Seeing the spark from a Sperm whales' eye flicker and die,
Knowing on that day I could not and would not fail.
For the veil of reality revealed a crack,
And behind the door I heard the cry.

The mind that dwells in the sea became known to me,
I received the gifts of protection and perception,
And cast away my allegiance to humanity,
Becoming a knight protector of the sea,
Loving her children without exception,
Defending them from human eco-insanity.

When in the grace of the sea, there is no danger,
The shroud of the ocean protects the defender,
And all those who serve under my command.
To the raging tempest I am not a stranger,
And there is no human foe to who I shall ever surrender,
Nor will I ever acquiesce to any human demand.

In this odyssey, the sea turtle has been my guide
Guiding my hand to strike a vengeful blow
Leading me to the cetacean killers upon the stormy main,
Chasing the pirate to the harbor where we did collide
And there I vanquished that evil foe,
Cleansing the sea of her foul bloody stain.

The Death of a Whale

Upon the billowing shroud of the sea, under a greyish cloud,
Thunder clouds taking shape, twenty leagues off Mendocino Cape,
The crescent moon had rose, and amongst the twinkling stars it froze.
And suddenly there came a whoosh, as the sea exploded with a breach,
A whale, a sperm, a cachalot, from the sea did rise, did blow and breach.
So close, so close, so very close,
Scarce within my reach.

It was a pleasant night in June, under a rather melancholy moon.
Caught in its teeth, six meters of giant squid, captured from beneath.
Leviathan and prey crashed back into the brine in a frothy spray.
I watched with enraptured awe, my crew and I, not a word could we say,
As this whale, this sperm, this cachalot, dove into the depths, dark and grey.
With a splashing bow he was gone,
Concluding the grim ballet.

The sun's morning glow gave cry to the sky with a loud, "There she does blow."
The whales, the sperms, the cachalots, all around us, they did swim and breach.
Through the greyish gloom we saw the approach of the grisly Goliaths of doom.
Nearer they came, these steel sheathed slayers of sweet sentient grace,
We children of Ahab watched them approach with fear upon our face.
Oh, how I despised them,
These loathsome slayers of grace.

We heard the thunderous shot; we saw the blood, as the dying whale fought,
In the dark blue sea, she thrashed in pain as bullets through her body lashed.
Her hot breath shot forth in a pinkish mist from this dying cachalot.
She arched her back in a twist and rolled in horrific pain,
To slaughter this wondrous armless Buddha was senselessly insane.
And I could not help but wonder,
How many others had they slain?

Like a sad quixotic knight, we raced our Zodiacs with another pod in sight,
My small boat through the waves did rip as we chased that evil ship.
The harpoon we blocked, as before that high foreboding bow we rocked.
Before us the whales, the sperms, the cachalot numbered a pod of eight,
Two young calves, five females with a large bull as their protective mate.
A family waylaid by chance
Could we avert their grisly fate?

In mortal fear, raced the whales, we followed with the monster on our rear.
That steely prow did glide over the tide, cleaving the sea like an axe.
The harpooner was grim, he aimed at my heart as I looked back at him.
He could not kill a whale, a cachalot, with our bodies in the way.
The Russian captain ran forward and to the harpooner had his say:
His finger sliced across this throat,
As he screamed for us to stay away.

Like a delicate shell my little boat rose upon a surging swell,
I was so near I could smell the fear in their vaporous breath.
I could see a spout misting the air, I heard the whalers shout.
I went surfing down into a trough when I heard that horrific sound
The deadly missile whistled near overhead and I quickly turned around.
And what I saw horrified me
As my heart began to pound.

Like a woman tortured by a heartless fiend, I heard her painful scream,
She rolled on the flood as a fountain of blood spurted from her side.
"My God," I cried, watching helplessly, as in convulsions she died.
Her hot blood spread like a malignant stain on the surface of the sea,
The largest whale turned to the right, six others turned left to flee.
His tail rose and came down hard,
As his saddened fluke slapped the angry sea.

Beneath me the Leviathan swam towards the whaler with the intent to ram,
The big gun was steady and they were ready, reloaded with a merciless dart.
I saw his eye breach the surface, I saw the gun and knew that he would die,
This whale, this sperm, this cachalot, face to face with a monster on the sea.
In shock I sat in my tiny boat as witness to cold-blooded murder on the sea.
In a fight most unfair he would die,
Slaughtered on that sullen sea.

At point-blank range the gun did spit, a roar shook the air, as his body sank,
Slowly into the scarlet waters he bellowed, crazed with rage.
My tears did flow as the whalers smirked and shock vanquished all my fears.
This whale, this sperm, this cachalot, this savaged lord of the deep abyss,
Slain by ignorant black hearted nameless men, spineless and merciless –
Devoid of empathy, these killers on the sea,
Unmoved by the whales' distress.

In horror I sat, until suddenly I caught the whale's penetrating eye,
I looked at him and he looked at me and then he dove beneath the sea.
Aghast, I saw a trail of bloody bubbles coming towards me fast.
The whale, the sperm, this cachalot, rose from the sea and towered by our side,
My first thought was that this great titan would slay me before he died,
His teeth so close, his breath upon my face,
Steaming, streaming blood, cascading down his side.

Leviathan, his strength is great, and thus he has no need to hate.
I saw in his eye that he understood, that we were there for his good,
Reflected in that great whale's eye, I saw myself, a-scrying for a reason why.
Slowly he sank into the dark depths, I watched him sink beneath the shroud,
Rain like tears upon me fell, beneath a towering thundercloud.
All was quiet on the sea,
As blood oozed up from that darkened shroud.

Amidst the violence and the strife, he had chosen to spare my life.
With relief and great emotion, I sat in that boat upon the heaving ocean.
That eye, that eye, so beautiful and so real, oh my God it haunts me still;
Before he sank and departed, a message to me was imparted.
Repay this debt for your life, your course has now been newly charted.
You live to serve a greater good,
You must finish what you started.

That large orb, that sacred eye, like a sponge, my soul it did absorb.
The whale, the sperm, the cachalot, had struck my heart with one desire,
In its depths, I saw the past, felt the present, saw the future in that living glass.
On that spot I quit the maddening insanity of ruthless humanity.
I swore in a frustrated fit of angry profanity,
To forsake myself from
Mankind's festering inhumanity.

The dark and deep enchanted depths, does its silent secrets keep.
Benthic vows un-recanted, weigh heavily on the heart and mind,
The whale's hot blood still burns my soul and through desire drives my will
The whales, the sperms, the cachalots guide my hand on sea and land,
For in their service I am committed, and in their service, I do stand.
As the seas I have charted
Keep me sailing o'er the darkening sand.

- October 13, 2013
From the South Pacific Ocean

This incident took place in June 1975 some
60 miles off the coast of Cape Mendocino, California.

Ask Not for Whom the Whales Bleed They Bleed for Thee!

Cruising with anger through ribbons of sleet,
The ships push on through the freezing tempest,
Pursuing the Japanese whaling fleet.

For six weary years this battle has raged,
Fought upon a worldwide media stage,
Both sides engaged and bitterly enraged.

In distant dark waters cold and remote,
Punished by piercing howling Banshee winds,
In Southern oceans where the icebergs float.

The coldest of seas receives the hottest blood,
In the dark frigid waters, it flows,
Pouring off sad decks in a scarlet flood.

The world's greatest minds scream in abject pain,
They die before eyes devoid of pity,
Eyes that see profit in the crimson rain.

Thrashing in agony on the surface,
Spouting boiling blood in scarlet fountains,
Flesh melted by the merciless furnace.

Armored black hearts dismiss their fiery pain,
All that they ponder is what they will gain,
And thus, has humanity gone insane.

Against this foul arrogance we throw our rage,
Sailing into harms way to save the whales,

Eco-pirates born of another age.

Sailing against winds of opposition,
Weathering vicious and vile contempt,
Seeking the whale killers abolition.

Ships are rammed, scuttled, boarded and sunk,
The bullets fly and missiles are exchanged,
Into chilling seas, the small boats spill and dunk.

What is this obsession we can't resign?
Why do we care when the world turns away?
Is there any reason or grand design?

The whales close their eyes when the harpoon sings,
They kiss goodbye to the miracle of life,
Puzzled by the apes with the deadly stings.

Men who inflict cruel death without remorse,
Whaling this loathsome task, hellishly dark,
Men astride an apocalyptic horse.

Armed with the most lethal of evil spears,
Plunged into flesh so sensitive and warm,
Their screams fall upon insensitive ears.

Sparkles of scarlet dance in the salt mists,
The sea churns violent swells of crimson pain,
Justified by the lies of scientists.

To describe the horror this inspires,
Is not a task that mere words can perform,
The blood of the whales feeds these vampires.

Our dream is to drive a stake through their hearts,
Destroying their industry forever,
Of their culture of death, we wish no part.

We come as chariots riding the storm,
In the name of the three laws of nature,
We seek to force the poachers to conform.

Black samurai harpooning gentle whales,
These neurotic narcissistic ninjas,
Lethally impaling pregnant females.

The gentle giants of the deep blue sea,
Mysterious, magnificent and real,
Before mankind's evil they cannot flee.

Up from the sea an iceberg cobalt blue,
Reflects the dim light of the Southern Cross,
Thrilling each member of our gallant crew.

Each one of them have come from far and wide,
Ready to risk their lives for the great whales,
Weathering the winds, the swells and the tide.

Circling around the floating abattoir,
Tossing stinking, rotten, foul, butter bombs,
High seas comedic drama, très noir.

We are myth weavers on the dark oceans,
Inspired by Leviathan's sad song,
Guided by such powerful emotions.

We must not leave nothing to chance but chance,
We inspire our own realities,
Enhancing all our chances to advance.

I close my eyes to glimpse nature's stern face,
Feeling the music of this wondrous sphere,
Safe in the protection of her embrace.

The lord of death no longer makes me weep,
My eyes have gone bone dry of mortal tears,
We live now with promises we must keep.

We can no longer afford to lament,
The lives of whales we save sustains our souls,
Yet we are so far from being content.

We must approach with tempered violence,
Fighting a war with patience and restraint,
Not for us, passivity and silence.

I am the Captain and thus in command,
The lives of so many lie in my hands,
At my command they will defend and stand.

The tactics we deploy could be tragic,
But I know that shall never be the case,
None but whales shall die in the Antarctic.

It was there in the dying eye of a whale,
A promise made and a promise tested,
A promise that we cannot, must not fail.

The salty seas sing a deep mournful tune,
Warning that collapse may come very soon,
Bringing death to immortal old Neptune.

How does the briny ocean suffer death?
We all know the answer to that question,
We all die when the seas take their last breath.

Our species has become a multitude,
A viral plague upon this blue white pearl,
Soon our cities will witness solitude.

The green eyes of Princess Cassandra plea,
Begging the world to heed her dark warning,
This is a disaster we cannot flee.

The whales are the guardians of the future,
If they die, the oceans die, thus we die,
It's hope that we are working to secure.

In this gallant effort we take chances,
Change is brought about by profound courage,
Their Achilles heel is their finances.

We speak the language of economics,
It's the only language they understand,
Cutting kill quotas dictates our tactics.

Sailing into harm's way for the great whales,
Tens of Thousands of miles in pursuit,
Riding the Cape Rollers through raging gales.

What will end this mindless insanity?
When will they stop tormenting the great whales?

Whaling – this disgrace of humanity.

Sometimes it takes pirates to save the day,
Rules must be bent and a fine edge walked,
We fight to prevent the oceans decay.

We mount cameras instead of cannon,
Replacing bullets with digital chips,
Learning new ways to defend Poseidon.

Playing the silly new media game,
Print replacing old powder magazines,
Television thriving on fame and shame.

Harnessing McLuhan to our affairs,
Disciples of the rules of media,
Ignoring craven critics in armchairs.

There are many factions to consider,
So many strategies to contemplate,
Paths both hypocritical and bitter.

Truth is just a complexity of lies,
Spun by cyber whores on computer screens,
The story leads best that bleeds, screams and dies.

But beneath the sham of shameless posers,
Is the truth that we each hold in our hearts,
And no hearts are blacker than the whalers.

To our own species we may be traitors,
And very proud traitors we are indeed,
Condemned by cultural inquisitors.

Where this will ever end I have no clue,
We do what we do, that's all we can do,
As we pursue killers on the deep blue.

It's not just the whales, it's the vast ocean,
We cannot surrender this living prize,
Guided by fair reason and emotion.

In the end it is our strong love of life,
Our utmost respect for the living sea,
That gives us the strength to endure such strife.

Knights of Poseidon

There are some who say that the battle is over,
There are some who say this war can't be won.
There are some who say that it is a losing cause,
That we will never silence the harpoon gun.

But the only causes worth fighting for are the lost ones,
And we cannot surrender, or from this battle retreat.
We have no choice but to carry on,
We must never accept the possibility of defeat.

We shall continue to slam into the sides of the great whaling ships,
We must never surrender to those who kill the whale,
If the whales die, the oceans die and if the oceans die, we all die,
And if we love our children we cannot, must not fail.

For thirty-five years I have fought in this global war,
Fighting Norwegians, Icelanders, Japanese and Danes,
On the beaches of Siberia or amongst the icebergs of Antarctica,
Opposing guns, harpoons, clubs, ships and planes.

I once looked into a whale's dying eye,
The shame reflected in that eye haunts me still,
For the blame cannot fall on the heads of a few,
It's become part of our collective human will.

With hominid ruthlessness we plunder the seas
Taking all, more than we should, more than we need.
Where will it end? How can we save even ourselves?
With millions more mouths every year to feed.

We must harness the arrogance to challenge the ignorance,
Or our greed will rob the world of nature's magic,
And such a loss will be eternally tragic,
And our hearts will be broken, and our souls diminished.

I am fighting in a war that seemingly has no end,
Where victories are short lived and defeats are permanent,
From those who began this fight I remain the sole survivor,
Some have died, others resigned, and the rest rendered impotent.

Holding the promise, I saw in that eye, I have remained unscathed,
Despite this protection, my trident must be passed on,
And so, I wait for a man or woman to see what I saw in that dying eye.
For the time is nigh to initiate a new knight for Poseidon.

Odyssey for the Whales

This poem was written during in January 2007
during Operation Migaloo off the coast of Antarctica

My voyage has no end in sight,
Over three decades I've been in this fight,
The curse is upon me and cannot be lifted,
Into an infinite undercurrent I've sadly drifted,
There is no sweet surrender or retirement for me,
Without falling from grace with the heavenly sea.

From the day I looked into that whales' solitary eye,
Hearing and feeling that agonizing cry,
Choice was lifted for alternative plans,
To travel far too many foreign lands,
To the sea I go, and to the sea I serve,
The path is straight without a curve.

I want to, need to, desire to rest,
Every campaign is a deadly test,
From fight to fight never-ending
Always healing, always mending,
Every campaign could be the last time,
Why is saving lives such a horrible crime?

On the day that I was knighted by the divine gale,
I knew that in my battles I could not fail,
Nor could I, or my crew, be hurt or fall.
Magic yes, that was the call,
A truth felt in the deep depths of my soul,
True, only if I keep true to my role.

The power was once so much stronger,
Will it hold true for very much longer?
Findings paths where trails don't exist
Engaging foes in the storms and the mist,
Draped in a cloak of flowing mystery,
Allowing me to weave myth with history.

Shepherd avenger on the storm-tossed wave,
So many species, so many lives to save,
A madness of directed obsession,
Into the wind I scream my confession.
They know not what they do the fools,
I know I can stop them, if given the tools.

A fair ship and a brave crew,
Although good crew are so relatively few
The obstacles increasingly grow
Yet the power continues to flow,
And as it does, I must act at will,
Or all that I love they will surely kill

Within the dark confines of my inner being
It is from there that I perfected the art of seeing,
Seeing is treason to humanity
For what is revealed is mass insanity
Thus, all rules are broken in this quest,
No more must I regret or confess.

The sea, the mother sea, is everywhere,
And from her heart, rare mysteries I share.

Within her bosom I grow in strength,
I cannot leave her for any length.
Her beauty is perfect, her strength supreme,
Harsh the reality, gentle the dream.

The Siren of Sirens came last year,
She was all the beauty that I could ever fear,
Her song bewitched me to the point of diminishment,
She twisted me into her slavish instrument,
Her teasing deceit took me from Sedna's grace,
I surrendered to her song and her angelic face.

A face that was but a mask where deceit did weep
Beneath her beauty demons were asleep,
A vampire unconsciously feeding on magic, set to destroy,
Tossing me aside like a throw away toy,
Yet her song both chills and warms my heart still,
Although she nearly enslaved me to herself serving will.

I struggled to take on the Goliaths of doom,
Saw their blood-stained hulls emerge from the gloom,
The scream of the whales ran again in my ears,
From over the waves I could feel their fears.
Once again, the intimidating chase
It was away from stalking death that we did race.

My ear, assaulted by the song of the Siren, was shattered,
The song screamed that she was all that mattered,
No drug, no temptation could match her alluring voice,
It took all my strength to make my only choice,
Turning away hurt more than I would have thought,
But death was the price, if I had not.

Ahead of me the ice lies unwelcome and cold,
The babies that I once saved have grown old,
But in their eyes, I see gratitude
And it is that glimpse that shapes my evolving attitude,
I love them each and every one
From no creature in the sea would I shun.

I feel the movement of the shark,
As my ship glides over the waters dark,
And sad is the fate of the whale should we fail,
The odyssey may end in death or jail,
It matters only if the seas grace is mine,
Within her grace, all is well and fine.

My Siren has been set free from my snare,
For with her I must be true and fair.
For what she was to me, I was to her as well,
If I had fallen, she also would have fell,
So, in the end we both grow stronger,
And to each other be Sirens no longer.

Why do two souls wrestle in the gloom?
Is love always on a path to doom?
What is it that causes us to attract?
Do we simply envy those who have what we lack?
I must believe that there is something more.
I need to believe that we can open any door.

I love my Siren, but I love the sea more,
She loves me, but loves music more.
In the ocean of my life she is my tropical isle,
Where my dreams can rest in Utopian style,
I wish her well as she sings her dreams,
May my mother the sea protect her from demonic schemes.

For this I know and I know it true,
There are amongst us with magic so few,
Children of Sea and of Earth,
Empowered by nature from our birth,
When we meet we burn each other with our pain,
Lessons splashed upon our souls in a passionate stain.

Sometimes we are simply not ready to embrace,
And that is a tragedy for the human race,
For only the tortured can save the day,
Only the tormented can feel the way,
Alone and lost we seek the path to salvation,
Knowing that redemption is our final station.

I am on an oceanic Odyssey that never sights port,
Doomed to trials and tribulations of every sort.
But some day I will reach those infinite gates,
And beyond that the rest lies with nature's fates,
But looking back one final time,
I will see that in many ways our songs did rhyme.

Trials of a Whale Warrior

Cruising with anger through ribbons of sleet,
The ships push on through the freezing tempest,
Pursuing the Japanese whaling fleet.

For six weary years this battle has raged,
Fought upon a worldwide media stage,
Both sides engaged and bitterly enraged.

In distant dark waters cold and remote,
Punished by piercing howling Banshee winds,
In Southern oceans where the icebergs float.

The coldest of seas receives the hottest blood,
In the dark frigid waters, it flows,
Pouring off Jap decks in a scarlet flood.

The world's greatest minds scream in abject pain,
They die before eyes devoid of pity,
Eyes that see profit in the crimson rain.

Thrashing in agony on the surface,
Spouting boiling blood in scarlet fountains,
Flesh melted by the merciless furnace.

Armored black hearts dismiss their fiery pain,
All that they ponder is what they will gain,
And thus, has humanity gone insane.

Against this foul arrogance we throw our rage,
Sailing into harms way to save the whales,
Eco-pirates born of another age.

Sailing against winds of opposition,
Weathering vicious and vile contempt,
Seeking the whale killers abolition.

Ships are rammed, scuttled, boarded and sunk,
The bullets fly and missiles are exchanged,
Into chilling seas, the small boats spill and dunk.

What is this obsession we can't resign?
Why do we care when the world turns away?
Is there any reason or grand design?

The whales close their eyes when the harpoon sings,
They kiss goodbye to the miracle of life,
Puzzled by the apes with the deadly stings.

Men who inflict cruel death without remorse,
Whaling this loathsome task, hellishly dark,
Men astride an apocalyptic horse.

Armed with the most lethal of evil spears,
Plunged into flesh so sensitive and warm,
Their screams fall upon insensitive ears.

Sparkles of scarlet dance in the salt mists,
The sea churns violent swells of crimson pain,
Justified by the lies of scientists.

To describe the horror this inspires,
Is not a task that mere words can perform,
The blood of the whales feeds these vampires.

Our dream is to drive a stake through their hearts,
Destroying their industry forever,

Of their culture of death, we wish no part.

We come on chariots riding the storm,
In the name of the three laws of nature,
We seek to force the poachers to conform.

Black samurai harpooning gentle whales,
These neurotic narcissistic ninjas,
Lethally impaling pregnant females.

The gentle giants of the deep blue sea,
Mysterious, magnificent and real,
Before mankind's evil they cannot flee.

Up from the sea an iceberg cobalt blue,
Reflects the dim light of the Southern Cross,
Thrilling each member of our gallant crew.

Each one of them have come from far and wide,
Ready to risk their lives for the great whales,
Weathering the winds, the swells and the tide.

Circling around the floating abattoir,
Tossing stinking, rotten, foul, butter bombs,
High seas comedic drama, très noir.

We are myth weavers on the dark oceans,
Inspired by Leviathan's sad song,
Guided by such powerful emotions.

We must not leave nothing to chance but chance,
We inspire our own realities,
Enhancing all our chances to advance.

I close my eyes to glimpse nature's stern face,
Feeling the music of this wondrous sphere,
Safe in the protection of her embrace.

The lord of death no longer makes me weep,
My eyes have gone bone dry of mortal tears,
We live now with promises we must keep.

We can no longer afford to lament,
The lives of whales we save sustains our souls,
Yet we are so far from being content.

We must approach with tempered violence,
Fighting a war with patience and restraint,
Not for us, passivity and silence.

I am the Captain and thus in command,
The lives of so many lie in my hands,
At my command they will defend and stand.

The tactics we deploy could be tragic,
But I know that shall never be the case,
None but whales shall die in the Antarctic.

It was there in the dying eye of a whale,
A promise made and a promise tested,
A promise that we cannot, must not fail.

The salty seas sing a deep mournful tune,
Warning that collapse may come very soon,
Bringing death to immortal old Neptune.

How does the briny ocean suffer death?
We all know the answer to that question,

We all die when the seas take their last breath.

Our species has become a multitude,
A viral plague upon this blue white pearl,
Soon our cities will witness solitude.

The green eyes of Princess Cassandra plea,
Begging the world to heed her dark warning,
This is a disaster we cannot flee.

The whales are the guardians of the future,
If they die, the oceans die, thus we die,
It's hope that we are working to secure.

In this gallant effort we take chances,
Change is brought about by profound courage,
Their Achilles heel is their finances.

We speak the language of economics,
It's the only language they understand,
Cutting kill quotas dictates our tactics.

Sailing into harm's way for the great whales,
Tens of Thousands of miles in pursuit,
Riding the Cape Rollers through raging gales.

What will end this mindless insanity?
When will they stop tormenting the great whales?
Whaling – this disgrace of humanity.

Sometimes it takes pirates to save the day,
Rules must be bent and a fine edge walked,
We fight to prevent the oceans decay.

We mount cameras instead of cannon,
Replacing bullets with digital chips,
Learning new ways to defend Poseidon.

Playing the silly new media game,
Print replacing old powder magazines,
Television thriving on fame and shame.

Harnessing McLuhan to our affairs,
Disciples of the rules of media,
Ignoring craven critics in armchairs.

There are many factions to consider,
So many strategies to contemplate,
Paths both hypocritical and bitter.

Truth is just a complexity of lies,
Spun by cyber whores on computer screens,
The story leads best that bleeds, screams and dies.

But beneath the sham of shameless posers,
Is the truth that we each hold in our hearts,
And no hearts are blacker than the whalers.

To our own species we may be traitors,
And very proud traitors we are indeed,
Condemned by cultural inquisitors.

Where this will ever end I have no clue,
We do what we do, that's all we can do,
As we pursue killers on the deep blue.

It's not just the whales, it's the vast ocean,
We cannot surrender this living prize,

Guided by fair reason and emotion.

In the end it is our strong love of life,
Our utmost respect for the living sea,
That gives us the strength to endure such strife.

Destroying the Cetacean Death Star

The screams of dying whales fill my heart with pain?
The hottest of blood in the sea beckons me.
We must clean this foul sea of the human stain
The Cetacean Death Star shall no longer flee

The time has come the Walrus cried to talk of many things
Of strategy and tactics to end her loathsome career
And to restore these seas once again to their rightful kings
Time to place our words and actions before our mortal fear.

Dare we few begin our dance with history?
In black steel armor we so boldly advance
Ours is not a war for wealth and vain glory
It is for the life of whales we make our stance

We cannot, must not, will not, hesitate in our advance
Our focus narrowed to the destruction of the Star
The killing machine must not be given a second chance
If we all act boldly, hard and fast, they will not get far

What care we for consequences while whales die
There are so, so many humans, so few whales
Stop the Nisshin, save the whales! – Our battle cry
We must weigh our actions on nature's own scales

Into the cold dark sea of death, voyage the forty-eight
One small ship against a dangerous, ruthless killing fleet.
Our deadly enemy sponsored by the Japanese state
Destroying intelligence for mercury tainted meat

By saving the whales we can save our oceans
And thus, the salvation of humanity
Nothing will come from political motions
Greed has evolved into gross insanity

How do I even begin to communicate the loss?
These wise armless Buddha's are the very soul of the sea
Their loss cannot be measured in material or cost
It will be sad grief beyond measure for thee and for me

There is a conscious mind in the dark deep blue
Meditation, imagination, dreams, yes dreams
Love, romantic, maternal, paternal – true.
Beyond the foul evil of hominid schemes

We kill without empathy, pity, awareness or thought
Raping the innocent, spilling blood so hot, and so pure.
Destroying the Cetacean Death Star
It is this dark malignant force that we have always fought
Seeking sweet solace, seeking redemption, seeking a cure.

Go great whales; flee before the horrid sins of man
How can we look upon your form without shame?
We, the killer angel invaders from land
We, who look upon life as a divine game,

How can we redeem ourselves for our crimes against nature?
Primitive minds blessed with a genius for technology

We are so far below the nobility of their stature
Where they have enlightenment, we have just theology

I hear their voices in my dreams every night
Dark delirium gives way to desire
Destruction's destiny is here within our sight
Death can be cheated with passionate fire

We go forth like armored knights intent on nature's quest
The Midnight sun flashes fire on our ebony greaves
The sang real of Leviathan calls us to this test
Around us myth, truth, lies, legend and destiny swirls and weaves

Whale riders, shepherds and warriors raising swords
The frail shield of David reflecting glory
The powerful song of the whale strikes the chords
We must, we must, write an end to this story

Arrogantus ignoramus homo natura, we are
Cetus rex a mare morte unless, unless, unless,
We deliver a fatal blow after coming so far
We must depart this field with victory and with success

The Cetacean death star's foul carnage must end
Do we risk it all, our ship, ourselves and all?
Never before has such great risks been taken
In the service of another specie's call

Whales, wherefore arte thou swimming in this sea of ice and steel?
Opposing Mandelas overlapping, fired by emotion
Armor clashing with armor, tearing, grinding, screeching shrill
A battle between life and death upon this Southern Ocean.

Fighting Whalers in the Great Southern Ocean

I'm bound away, across the Great Southern Ocean,
In search of a horrific evil so violent,
Heeding the agonizing screams of dying whales,
My heart is bursting with conflicting emotion,
We have no choice, we cannot, must not, be silent,
Desperate actions are needed when all else fails.

We grow weary of the sad political games,
Useless bureaucrats posturing promises grand,
Rendering the possible so impossible
Contributing greatly to our collective shame
Japan, Norway, Denmark, Canada and Iceland
Five whale killing nations so irresponsible

We stand against a most violent powerful foe
A small band of pirates against an empire
A passionate compassionate crew very bold
Heading southward where the Antarctic ice does floe
Where perverse men suck whale blood like a vampire
Slaughtering life in the oceans for pride and gold.

The *Nisshin Maru* is the cetacean death star
Sending out killers to slay the gentle giants
Spilling the hottest of blood into the cold sea
Where is my bold support crew from Madagascar?
We need to throw all we have at their arrogance
These killers have ignored Australia's civil plea.

They are criminal poachers, just simple and plain
Yakusa sponsored amakudari corruption
Just arrogant outlaws acting above the law

In a world oblivious to the whale's great pain
How to deal with humanity's great contradiction?
And international law enforcements great flaw?

We must act now where all others fear to do so
We must uphold the law against these ruthless killers
Is it arrogant to challenge their arrogance?
Taking action to defeat this merciless foe
As their evil propaganda become shriller

I have spent an entire lifetime fighting whalers,
Hunting, ramming, sinking, destroying their foul ships,
Portugal, Spain, Iceland, Norway and now Japan
A lifetime of victories and sometimes failures
Enduring heavy seas, loneliness and hardships
In our quest to uphold the whaling ban.

- December 2009

Guarding the Southern Gates

Where oh where have all the whaling ships gone?
Southward they slowly come from far Nippon,
We wait for them to arrive at our gate,
These mad murderers from a corrupt state.

They stole Tsunami funds from the homeless,
With a great evil intent to transgress,
To the Southern sea to murder the whale,
It is our intent to see that they fail.

Oh pardon me gentle beast of the seas,
That I am gentle with thugs such as these,
We will intercept their nautical course,
And we will challenge their cruel lethal force.

We intervene without inflicting hurt,
Their brutal harpoons we aim to avert,
We do what we must because others won't,
When we do what we do, they tell us don't.

But it matters not what our critics say,
We are in the Southern Ocean to stay,
Our noble mission is to save the whale,
With no intention to retreat or fail.

They call us racists for saving the whale,
Desperately pulling that card when they fail,
Like thieves these craven killers approach,
Intently seeking endangered whales to poach.

Most nations bow to their wealthy demands,
Continuing to shake their blood-stained hands,
They harness the media to spread their lies,
Demonizing us under Southern skies.

They buy sell sword lawyers to run us down,
I narrowly escaped that German town,
Slimy tentacles so deadly and long,
Despite this we stand guard both tall and strong.

My Crew Envisioned in the Eye of My Whale

What kind of men and women are on this crew?
Who are these rare and caring and fearless few?
Charging forth for the whales on the deep dark blue.

Before silent eyes, inspiration breaches,
Ripples of life lap upon the world's beaches,
Blessed are all the students the whale teaches.

Knowledge is a shape rising from the Oceans,
Leviathan's eye reveals our emotions,
Whale tears - the most potent of salty potions.

That solitary eye into my eye peered.
There the image of all my sins lay mirrored.
My destiny was everything that I feared.

Strange whale magic worked upon my fate that day,
A breaching transcendence was put into play,
Placed on a straight path from which I could not stray.

Melville wrote we are enveloped in whale lines,
Truth from the eye of the whale forever shines,
For upon my soul karma forever dines.

Death had caught me up in a swift sudden turn,
Silent, subtle, perils of life I did learn,
As God upon an ocean of blood did churn.

We cannot seduce the enemies we fear,
We defeat the enemy with a mirror,
Eye to eye, boldly defending flank and rear.

Pursuit, intervention, skirmish, deception.
Prepared with changing tactics of reception,
No compromise, no retreat, or exception.

Victory is obtained by the strength of will,
Resolve and persistence are the daily drill,
Wearing the enemy down before the kill.

Our resolve gives us invincibility,
We possess the strength and the ability,
Our advantage is their vincibility.

The fiery blue ice can be friend or foe,
Patience, we take it easy, we take it slow,
We feel our way through the treacherous ice floe.

Onward, ever onward, we voyage for weeks,
The freezing salt lashing and kissing our cheeks
The red paint of our hull stains the ice in streaks.

Grinding, crashing, smashing, rolling slabs of ice,
Every turn of the wheel is like rolling dice,
With cold dark death we flirt, we dance and entice.

This voyage is merely another chapter,
In a book of decades fighting disaster,
And to these events the whale was the master.

Guiding and protecting in every campaign,
Avoiding death, injury, prison and pain,
Cleansing the living sea of the human stain.

There is magic here beyond comprehension,
That does remove both fear and apprehension,

There is no burden of worry or tension.

Ahab's sad fate was to personify hate,
To him nature was his, to rape and to take,
In loving nature, we eradicate hate.

Karmic law is a very fine line to walk,
Guided by real emotions and not by talk,
Sensitive to each karmic tremor and shock.

Balancing actions on a delicate scale,
Intuition is the guide that must not fail,
Integrity must be the most blessed grail.

Saints for nature are most exceedingly rare,
Satanic Pan is unleashed as Christians stare,
Virtues of humanity are quite unfair.

We who have seen truth in the eyes of a whale,
Wear a rare veil of armour that cannot fail.
Our truth, our cross, is the whale's powerful tail.

So difficult to explain in words and verse,
This odyssey that has been blessing and curse,
Within this new paradigm we are the first.

In all of human history, no one has dared,
To risk all for those whose world we have shared,
History will record that we truly cared.

That great whale who spoke to me so long ago,
In whose body the hottest of blood did flow,
He envisioned the long path that we would go.

Oh Leviathan, hallowed be thy name,
Thy will shall be done.

- January 15th 2009

Snow

Mother nature standing tall in the south,
Unfolds her misty white apron.
Sweet whispers issued from her mouth,
Breathing from horizon to horizon.

She shakes loose her apron over the sea,
The soft white crystals slowly fall,
On the head of Persephone.
Thus, her loving daughter hears her soft call.

Quietly descending, pretty and slow,
From the fluffy ivory skies,
Upon the salt sea falls the snow,
With frozen tears, Gaia quietly cries.

Each tear is a singular work of art,
Each individually crafted,
Flakes off a mother's gentle heart,
Descending silently, rising wafted.

Alabaster blankets smother the land,
Tears changing into crystal gems,
Droplets of tears form mountains grand,
Whispering poems, singing silent anthems.

- February 19th, 2010

The Curse of Ahab's Children

They entered the Sanctuary the hour before dawn
A deadly greasy fleet of grisly death, searching for innocent prey
Elusive, menacing, efficiently ruthless, and terribly swift and fast.
Harpoon guns screaming like Banshees throughout the long summer's day,
Crouching in killing stances before their bleeding rigid mast,
Sentient awareness expiring with each horrific harpoon's thundering blast.
Waiting for the word of law from the world, we held back our attack,
But word of law from the world never came,
Lawlessness has been bartered for hypocritical trade,
The governments have betrayed the whales once again in deceitful shame,
Posturing, talking, spouting hot air, breaking every promise made,
Apathy and inaction, rising, as the integrity of compromised politicians fade.
Condemnation for those of us who sail to defend life,
Accusations of terrorism against us from vicious merciless killing machines,
The Japanese death ships bent and intent upon inflicting unbearable pain,
Ships of steel softer than the heart of their crews of murdering fiends,
From their decks of steaming gore, the hot blood of Leviathan does drain
Into the frigid dark blue sea leaving a scarlet warm, obscene steaming stain.
Softly we navigate through the treacherous twisted ice, crossing their deadly path.
Blocking, harassing, intervening, protecting and defending the gentle giants.
Frustration mounting as harpoons thunder and innocent whales scream,
Reminding ourselves that it is the whales who are our clients,
We cannot care, nor be influenced by the hypocrisy of this human scheme
We have to take action to stop these blood mad killers by any non-lethal means.
Killing for research is killing plain and simple,
Killing for research is the legacy of the Nazi and Togo's barbaric Japan,
There is no place in this new century for such vicious meddling,
Japan has slaughtered tens of thousands of whales since the world whaling ban
Lying about research to cover the whale meat they are peddling.
Pretending to deceive the world with the outrageous lies they are peddling.
Must we sacrifice our lives to awaken the world to this disgrace?
Must we toss away our freedom in this effort to stop this bloody slaughter?
What will it take for governments to uphold the rule of law?

We have no choice but to take a stand for every son and daughter
Why must we endure such hell because the law has this serious flaw?
The flaw that trade can dictate discrimination in the enforcement of the law.
We care not what our critics say we are, we do not fight upon the seas for them.
We fight for our friends, the whales against the most evil of blood thirsty foes.
We drive our ship to the Southern seas to defend the defenseless from the remorseless,
We drive our ship towards the place where the hottest of blood floes
We go into battle against killers cruel, hardened and merciless.
For in the end, what matters is that we stand for justice.
The steely Antarctic skies go on forever
We risk our lives to allow the whales to also live forever,
We cannot sit upon our ass, doing nothing as these gentle creatures die,
Action in defense of life is the standard by which our lives must be measured.
We fight against cruelty, against death and against the Japanese lie,
Seeking to stop the flow of blood, under the frozen Southern sky.
All of us are Ahab's children.
The death of millions of whales blights our history and our souls,
The least we can do to expunge this awesome burden and curse
Is to drive every existing whaling ship onto rocky shoals,
To attack their profits and empty every greedy whaler's purse
There can be no compromise and the whales must come first.
I know not what the future will bring,
I put my trust in my ship and my brave inspired crew,
Our task is formidable and our resources are small,
We are a band of warrior although few, we are a happy few,
And if in this battle, some of us do fall,
No one can say that we did not answer Leviathan's sad call.
The angels of the sea, the playful dolphins guide us,
From out of the horde of billions we few do rise and sail,
We are the children of Ahab now wedded to Moby's cause,
And for the whales, we will not, cannot, must not fail.
We do not fight for profit or for the world's applause
And thus, we hunt for the killers to uphold conservation laws.
Oh gentle, gentle Leviathan, most noble creature of the sea,

In our actions you will know that not all of humanity is cruel,
And we the children of Ahab, like knights with honour before you kneel,
We have chosen and decided that we will not be destruction's tool,
For deep in the depths of our outraged hearts, your pain we passionately feel,
As your song echoes and stirs our souls beneath our sturdy keel.
Our shepherd's staff of protection crossed with the trident of intervention,
We sail beneath the black flag of freedom on a righteous quest,
Our bow points towards confrontation and dangerous pursuits,
We have no choice to do anything else we must confess,
For the call of Migaloo echoes and grabs our attention by the roots,
We must stop that cowardly harpooner before once again he shoots.

The Death of a Whaler

Hajime Shirasaki came South with murder on his mind,
Karma has a way of turning gold into retribution
Betraying nature does provoke consequences for mankind
Karmic law commands a punitive mortal contribution

And thus poor Hajime died for the whaler's blasphemous sins
Servant to the Yakusa, slayer of the armless Buddha's
Enemy of the sweet sentient creatures of fluke and fin
Cowardly eta outcast, barbaric butchering Judas

A horrible way to die, screaming into the bitter wind
I wonder if the whales far below heard his frightened cries?
Did the Giant Petrel stare? Did the gliding Albatross grin?
Sliding beneath the silent shroud of the sea, sputtering lies.

The Southern Ocean has tales of woe that would make your blood freeze
And no tale is colder that watching the lights of your ship fade
As the cold opens every pore and ice water begins to tease
The dim stern light, is the last thing he ever saw, I'm afraid.

Hajime's tragic death gave the whales a day of exemption
The cruel sea taketh and giveth life as nature intended.
His death bought life for a day for the whales as just redemption.
The rich hot blood of man and whale, in fear and death, now blended

We sail each day through a sea filled with the wispy shadows of death.
Hellish harpoons of terror pluck life from the sea like ripe fruit
Dancing on wire over the frozen gorge of sudden death.
Demons are no protection when karma plays her righteous flute

Hajime the whaler rolls silently on this ruthless Ocean
The sad tears of his surviving crewmates are so much cheap salt
The ocean needs no more, absorbing death, without emotion
To come down here to inflict death and to die is one's own fault

Three whalers have died in this war over the fate of the whale
We have been spared tragedy by Sedna's benevolent grace
In this divine maritime comedy, karmic laws never fail
Death and misery, the rewards of the slayers in this chase

Icebergs stand as solemn silent tombstones for every whale slain
Frozen gardens of mammoth monuments of bluish white glass
Between these stones of water rush the criminally insane
Vicious harpoon cannons spitting violent death with every blast

Whales weep not for the fate of man for we are undeserving
Our iron clad hearts were torn from the soul of the Earth long ago
To this Earth very few have devoted their life to serving
And the masses have begun to reap the evil seed they sow

For centuries man has cruelly slaughtered the Mind in the Deep
The horror of whaling etches indelible stains on our souls
Whales screaming their death in our deaf ears as we dream in our sleep
The stench of their flesh dripping and sizzling on the hot coals

Hajime Shirasaki rest in peace on Sedna's soft breast
Karma has claimed you in atonement for your national sin
Sliding beneath the shroud of the sea, did you pray and confess?
Did you ask for redemption from the Buddha's of fluke and fin?

The Endless Quest

Adieu my darling, the whales of the sea are dying and we know why,
Slaughtered by pirates, we must follow their cry,
The engine hums, turns, moves slow, so far to go,
The cry of "T'har she blows" erupts, as hot blood from gaping wounds do flow.

The cold sea is so embarrassed for us, all certainties disappear,
We need only empty our sad hearts of fear,
We voyage so far, so very far from land,
To a so very lonely place, very lonely, where we make our stand.

A ship of heroes? Or a wise ship of fools? What is wrong? What is right?
People of peace forced into a complex fight,
In a crazy charge against insanity,
We are such a small insignificant fraction of humanity.

So many self-righteous cynics, so much hatred, selfishness and greed,
For humanity to grow, the world must bleed,
We can feel the anger, the fear and the hate,
Staring into the cold eyes of bureaucratic minions of the State.

The harpoons thunder, pierce, and explode in a fiery vicious rape,
Pantheistic shields repelling waves of hate,
Her dying screams echo darkly inside my mind,
Gasping, thrashing, in agonized horror at the cruelty of mankind.

Into this wild sea of slaughter, we voyage, sailing close hauled with the law,
Jagged open wounds torn, ragged, red and raw,
Humanity destroying life in God's name,
Cowards coveting blood money, searching for other species to blame.

Humanity has lost the desire to endure a selfless quest,
In serving this living Earth there is no rest,

Enduring ridicule and the ignorant jests,
Humankind has long forgotten that we remain temporary guests.

The magical nature of this voyage is shrouded in mystery,
The magic can be glimpsed in our history,
Upon this great black ship, we all are blessed,
Unless and except those whose treacherous natures remain unconfessed.

Tragedy has struck those few who have lied, sabotaged and betrayed,
Mediocrity followed those who have strayed,
Powers sprung forth from an unfathomable source,
We keep to our course guided by the light of this benevolent force.

Over the dark shroud of the sea we move, wedded to the tidal flood,
The rising moon provokes the salt in our blood,
Songs of whales vibrate the rhythm in our souls,
World changing songs transcending time, lapping on uncaring coral shoals.

Be'twixt the dimensions of reality defined by human thought,
Nature's world that humanity has long fought,
Imprisoned in our encyclopedia,
Replaced by the trivial hysteria of modern media.

Hypnotized by charismatic whores peddling utopian dreams,
Bread and media circuses masking schemes,
Truth is distorted to what they want to hear,
Manipulating mass movements to govern by false hope and by fear.

Willing the wind, waves, weather and currents to carry out her commands,
The spirits of the victims scream their demands,
Harnessing the strength of her intrepid knights,
To sally forth in forest, desert, plain and sea in a thousand fights.

Ahead lies violent death, inspired by the coal black heart of culture,

A ship that laps steaming blood like a vulture,
Three little killers with deadly little dicks,
Blowing holes in the holy mind of the sea for profit and for kicks.

Hominid cockroaches scurry evilly over mutilated whales,
Nations weigh decisions on corrupted scales,
Talk, the excuse for doing nothing at all,
Diplomacy, the justification for the Japanese to stall.

The resolute spirit of the samurai has long been laid to rest,
Seppaku, a mere step upon Sedna's breast,
Seaman swallowed by a cold blooded kraken,
A sacrifice, that the consciousness of Moana may awaken..

The albatross guides this fair black ship protected by a karmic shroud,
Southward under the land of the long white cloud,
Onward to the edge of the far Southern Sea,
As the whales flee from the deadly harpoons, the killers before us flee.

- January 23, 2009

The Sea Shepherd Crew

Oh, What kind of men and women are these,
That journey into such hostile seas?
Where the snow does fall, and the waters freeze,
So far from the land, so far from the trees.
Working long, hard, cold, hours without pay,
Risks, without the expectation of gain,
Selflessly defending the whale's domain,
Reducing the number of whales they slay.
The sanctuary must be defended,
This crew only acts when governments fail,
These arrogant whalers must be halted,
This criminal whaling must be ended,
They risk it all for the sake of the whale,
The sanctuary shan't be assaulted.

Nine years they've gone down to the southern sea,
With each year getting better and better,
With crossed staff and trident on their sweater
A single purpose with which they agree.
Pledging their lives to save so many lives,
Always careful not to harm the whalers,
In that intent there can be no failures,
Going to sea, so the species survives.
Why does this crew do this year after year?
What drives them to such a difficult task?
Who are these sailors who go south in ships?
Doing nothing is what this crew most fear,
And when anyone does bother to ask,
Love is the reason, read upon their lips.

Sanctuary does mean sanctuary,
Endangered are the Humpbacks and the Fins,
Old Ahab's death has not absolved their sins,
Thus cultures clash every January.
The whale killers are ruthless in their quest,
They hate the Sea Shepherds with a passion,
Failing to understand our compassion,
Or why their whale poaching we must suppress.
Merciless killers, so stubborn proud,
Self-proclaimed destructive angels of death,
Devoid of empathy, pity, and kindness.
Our brave crew unbowed, will never be cowed,
Determined to resist with every breath,
The sin of humanity's sad blindness.

The Tempest

This poem was written in January 2008 as the Steve Irwin sailed South to confront the Japanese whaling fleet. I wrote it during the storm in an attempt to capture the emotions of the crew and the groaning of the ship.

In confidence my ship sailed South,
Oblivious to danger,
I feared not the coming storm,
To such winds I was no stranger.

But amongst my crew were virgin sailors
Some still sea-sick from just the gentle motions,
For them I knew this would be a test,
And fear would dominate their emotions

The mild sea gave way to rising swells,
Whitecaps spit their salty spray
The swells did begin to rise with the tide,
And upon the dark shroud did flay,

The apprentices on the deck looked towards the rising clouds
Young eyes grew wide with growing apprehension.
Lightning crackled in the sky,
There was growing comprehension.

The tempest burst upon us like a bomb,
The wind plucked the lines in a deadly dearth
The winds wailed through the rigging,
And from dark clouds the storm gave birth.

With lightning flash, the rains did lash,
And scoured the decks completely clean,
The wind rose to a frightening roar,
And howled forth like a fiend.

Like a Banshee's mournful deadly wail,
The evil winds did taunt
Disturbing every dead sailor's bones
From the depths they rose to haunt.

Within the gale we heard them chuckle
The aquatic ghouls put on a grisly show
They sought for us to join them,
To share in their pitiful soggy woe

"Ignore the fiends," the Captain cried.
"Ignore the sultry Sirens to,
We shan't be joining them tonight,
No, not this gallant crew."

The ship did rock and it did roll,
Like a toy boat at the mercy of the gale,
Helpless we watched and kept the course,
Hoping the engines would not fail,

To drive into a Cyclone's maw,
Is to spit into God's merciless face,
Prayers and pleads are useless words,
When salt is all you taste.

The wind drives salt from your eyes,
It hurls brine into your frozen face,
Your skin it crawls with the crystals sharp,
This hell provides no safe place.

You watch the bow plunge and dive,
The sea assaults the lonely deck,
The hull it groans and the keel does shiver,
Terrified rats get set to jump the wreck,

The pounding increases as the winds rage on,
Glass is shattered, the lifeboats torn away,
The ship rolls and moans like a dying thing,
And the crew curses every minute of the day.

The savage winds rode on our stern,
The monstrous gale kicked us in our ass,
We surfed upon mountainous seas,
Yearning for the storm to pass.

Salted water flogged us like slaves
As we fought to keep the ship on course,
Blind and deaf we bent our backs,
My God what an awesome force!

Soaked and tired and frozen stiff,
Fingers numb and elbows sore,
Striving to stay awake and alert,
Thank God, we're far offshore.

I shudder to think what a reef would do,
Such winds would dash us to a crushing hell,
No rocks out here to strike a lethal blow,
Each roll does strike the bell.

Sailors tossed like rag dolls across the heaving sea,
She taunts and teases and scoffs at our displeasure.
Our moans and pains mean naught to her,
Her destruction knows no measure.

And as if to illustrate her rage,
She pelts us with hardened balls of hail,
Then slathers us with hoary rotten sleet,

As the gale continues to scream and wail.

And through the wind-blown rain I see,
Just how majestic her power emerges,
Admiration removes all fear,
And I hear the poetry in her howling dirges.

I smile and lick the salt from my lips,
Content to ride this storm to hell,
And in that moment the wind did sigh,
And a calm spread out upon the swell,

The sun pierced the dark grey clouds,
A golden ray did stab the deck and mast.
A rainbow struggled across the sky,
The storm was over at last.

Within hours calm was restored,
The recent past was like a dream,
The violence fled without regret,
From the drying deck rose steam.

A sailors first storm is a nightmarish thing,
Driving fear into the heart and soul,
Once over it reveals just how sweet life really is,
The enlightenment achieved is worth the fearful toll.

Whispering Southern Winds

I haunt the ice that overlooks the sea,
In the Southern summer the cold wind blows,
Blowing snow exposes the cold black stone,
Powdered gusts slide across the flowing ice,
Seals pop their puppy dog heads through black holes,
Eerie silence spreads across the waters,
Penguins stand like motionless sentinels,
Whales move like slowly rolling mandalas,
Broad white sashes spread across inky seas
I see the near future so clear and strange,
As briny tears freeze fast upon my cheeks,
As the horror from the North moves closer,
Bringing noise and the stench of diesel fumes,
Reaping grim death in profitable strokes,
Harpoons, hooks, longlines, rifles and seine nets,
Diamond drills penetrate the sea bottom,
Seismic guns basting sound into the earth,
Generator plants humming obscenely,
Muffling the silence with spinning turbos,
Coal spilling from raw wounds in the mountains,
Bleeding oil, gas and uranium,
Black dry rain coats the alabaster hills,
Rivulets of water drip, drip and drip,
Drop by steady drop the seas slowly rise,
Acid eats away the song of the whales,
Slowly, ever slowly they disappear,
Gargantuan nets scoop up plankton,
Stealing whale food to feed to tortured pigs,
Huge appetites draining the sea of life,
The weight of the top, crushing the bottom,
Humans flowing like wildfire southward,
Man swarm, the curse of civilization,
Evicting the many tribes of penguins,
Machinery rumbling over the ice and snow,
It cannot be, must not be, shall not be,
The great curse consuming all before it,
Africa, America, Australia.
And now remote and cold Antarctica,

Her great white shield shattered like frosted glass,
The Aurora Australis cries above,
Flickering blue, green, yellow and red,
I shake the horrific dream from my head,
The whale's graceful tail waves a sad farewell,
I smile and know what it is to die,
To feel just what it is to truly die!
Knowing that there is nothing left behind,
Corporate vampires have sucked it dry,
Sending penguin corpses to the museums,
Leaving the noisy shores silent of life.
White mountains will dissolve into the sea,
Black rocks will absorb the heat of the sun,
The eggs drop from very unhappy feet,
The Great Southern Ocean gives up her ghosts,
Their wails whistle through glittering white ribs,
Whispering haunting funeral dirges,
Wondering where the children have all gone.

- January 2013

Twilight and Rebirth
in the Great Southern Ocean

The midnight sunbeams were dancing over the waves out on the Southern Sea,
Icebergs sparkled like cobalt blue sapphires set in a tiara of profound majesty
A familiar voice echoed down the years, so haunting in its song
That voice that had chained me to the sea for so, so, very long.
Sweet melodic words that reminded me again that it is love that makes us strong,
Bonded by a curse of gratitude and a promise to right a shameful wrong,
The cold dry air wrapped tightly around me as I stood there on the wooden deck,
And looked in sullen sadness upon our loss, upon that sorry wreck,
Caught unaware we had been rammed and sunk by remorseless cold-blooded whaler men,
In a cowardly attack from the cold-hearted mercenary killers of hot-blooded Leviathan.
I stood upon the deck and listened to that siren's voice that I had once heard so long ago,
And thought of the wearisome battles I have fought for over thirty years or so,
You gave me little choice. In your debt, I nailed your colors to our mast,
Your death in the crosshairs of that ship of death, shattered by that harpoon blast.
For decades I have trusted in your wisdom, in your sacred truth to set me free,
Wandering in a martial manner across the stormy seas, degree after tedious degree.
My thoughts have traveled in bursts of light across the many turbulent years,
My life has been lived without doubts, without guilt and without normal mortal fears,
All those years of toil, of horror, of frustration, of anger and of strife,
And all the misery, the suffering, the pain, the disappointment and the loss of life,
Into the Pandorian eye of Poseidon I had gazed, searing my soul with a lingering pain,
Into the dark bluish black depths of the sea, I stare, searching for truth once again,
Across the grey shroud of the world's oceans I have fought darkness in your name,
Club and hook, net and harpoon, implements of death and hatred all the same,
Those hominid fiends who tore the beautiful wings from the aquatic angels,
And stripped their bleeding silken flesh for base gold and silver shekels.
I took their clubs, smashed their harpoons, destroyed their nets and hooks,
And documented the victories in film, photos, magazines and books,

Death was always pushed aside for you gave me your immortal shield,
And to my enemies and betrayers you forced them to desist, to die, and to yield,
You gave me your promise of protection from death and the forces of corruption,
And in return I have fought your quixotic battles without rest or interruption.
And now in this place as the carpet of the sea is swept clean with the hottest of tears,
And all the whales flee before the horror, their bodies chilled by unknown fears,
I have held your lofty banner, I have held it through victories over civilized insanity,
I never dropped it once during defeats in the face of human evil and depravity,
Your gift to me held true, no harm, no freedom lost, your love did make me strong.
The Southern gales carry your songs into the ear of my heart where they belong,
In closing my eyes, I see your pain, I see your sacrifice, I see my reflection in your eye.
As across the waves my fleet drives relentlessly forward as over the waves we fly.
My senses have been shattered and my soul has crept along the edge of madness,
She is harsh the sea, cold and merciless and a very savage enchantress.
Pursuers pursuing pursuers, grappling, boarding, blockading, ramming and rammed,
Shoved, shot, slandered, shattered, scattered, damned and slammed
Driving forward into blizzards, hurricanes and typhoons,
Pushing through ice and braving reefs in our quest to destroy the harpoons.
The troubled winds of fury have blown harsh and hot upon my face,
I wonder if I ever I will be allowed to retire alive from the sea with grace
Knowing that there is only one key to unlock the prison created by that oath I swore,
There can only be one way that I can drop the sword and retire from this endless war
In love is my salvation and it is love that bestows forgiveness
Allowing me to forsake the sword for the pen, my ships for happiness
To be saved from the cold embrace of the sea by the warm embrace of a wife
As the cold winds pass over me leaving me in the wake of this salty life of strife,
Forgive me Leviathan, for I have loyally served the seas as your warrior knight
But now I wish to, need to, desire to, and yearn to leave this fight
Even at the cost of my immortality, that is the gift I will freely sacrifice,
For love for her, for love I will pay the sea her price.
For I have held this aquatic banner, so very high, so very long and forever strong
Forever in the chambers of my heart echoes Leviathan haunting song,
And I have been given the chance to trade nature's magic for nature's love,
To seek out happiness on the land and in the hills above.

With pen I shall continue the fight for the courage of truth never can be retired,
And I will never abandon my allegiance to all that I've defended and admired,
But the time now has come to talk of other things,
Of commitment to another heart, to passionate love and symbolic rings
To creating in her little sea, a unification of she and of me,
Our gift for a better world, for a future we would like to see.

Verses Afloat Upon the Sea

A poem in a bottle tossed upon the stormy sea,
A message sent forth with hope for an answer back to me.
Where and to whom will the currents and tide bring my missive?
Will Wind and rocks and reef conspire to be dismissive.

A note in a wine bottle tossed into the cold Bering Sea,
Delivered an answer fifteen years later back to me,
Another in the warm Filipino Sulu Sea did fall,
Upon an Indonesian beach where coconut crabs fall.

Plucked from the heated sand by a fisherman's weathered hand,
The note promised a small reward from a far distant land.
I wonder how many bottles float on the briny flood?
And how many messages lie buried in benthic mud?

How many last wills and testaments are entombed in glass?
How many penned floating tragedies survive from the past?
Short notes in bottles are the last gasps of dying sailors,
All that remains of ship-wrecked merchants, warriors and whalers.

The most passionate of notes were those tossed upon the Main.
The most desperate of epistles written while in pain,
Sailors staring into the blackness of oblivion,
Fearful of dying, fearful of the unknown and beyond.

Lord George Byron tossed a cork bottled poem into the deep,
A note to fair sweet Loukas for whom he missed and did weep,
Poems and bottled notes are the legacy of sad passion,
All that remains after the eating of the last ration.

Delivery is dependent upon wind, current and tide,
Left to chance, fate and the abyss to reach the other side.
Is there a Buddhist prayer more sacred than a floating note?
Eternity can most plainly see what words have been wrote.

No other missive is so terribly open and bare.
Hope sends forth a message with chances of delivery rare.
Words naked under the elements, seasick with despair,
Dizzy words, drunk on the brine tainted befouled bottled air.

There is no lonelier note upon this great Earth, alas,
Than a message, a will, or verse, entombed in transparent glass.
Open to the radiant sun, and yet not seen nor read,
Words that scream forth with very painful desire to be said.

Words of love, of hopelessness, pleas for help, questions of science,
Unending odysseys and dying words of defiance,
Words broken upon far foreign beaches, oozing black ink,
Lost bottles containing lost promises that float or sink.

There are many deep secrets in our mother ocean's womb,
The seven seas do serve as library, museum and tomb,
Inside a scroll of glass, place and cork your verse or story,
Chance will lose it forever or transport it to glory

There is an art to placing notes in the vast open ocean,
Exceptions of course for cases of panicked emotion,
A natural cork preferred with a strong colored glass flask,
Acid free paper, and indelible ink for the task.

Set a course for the bottle with the current, wind and tide,
Once set free upon the sea your sacred message will ride,
Remember to include, position, address and date,
Throw it well clear of the ship's wake into the hands of fate.

Bottles can contain marvelous magical things its true.
Treasure maps, genies, riddles and spirits to name a few,
The greatest treasure of all are words tossed on a lonely beach,
Profound words, poetic words of passion that reach and teach.

All modern poets should entomb their words in colored glass,
Better to be lost forever on the storm-tossed flood,
Than ignored in a sad culture of apathy and mud,
Where arrogant ignorance chills the soul, freezes the blood.

When I am no more present in thought, memory, or form.
A part of me will still continue to weather the storm,
My few words will float until on a beach will someday land,
When a stranger's hand will pluck my words from the foam and sand.

Bottled messages are anxious genies seeking release,
Confessions begging for absolution from any priest.
Pathways and maps to riches for the very lucky few,
A bequeathing to the unknown by an unlucky crew.

A message in a bottle remains a symbol of hope,
Tying us to strangers with an immaterial rope,
There are very few sailors who have sailed the vast ocean,
Who have not posted letters at sea without emotion.

This very verse will be printed on a nautical chart,
Into a corked brown bottle, I will deliver my art,
To be thrown with great hope and wondrous loving emotion,
Into the cold dark embrace of the Great Southern Ocean.

WHALE WARS

Sent off by Neptune in Brisbane
In lightening and driving rain
Onboard a famous mermaid fair
To try and make the world aware

In Newcastle we stopped for fuel
In preparation for the duel
Then off to Taz and Hobart town
To prepare for another round

South, we pointed our bow once more
Far from Australia's secure shore
Looking for any signs of Whalers
The most evil of all sailors

Finally, through the fog and snows
A whaler emerged through the floes
We attempted to mount a raid
Plans to intercept were then made

The boat launched, the crew made ready
Rising seas made things unsteady
The swells rose, the winds increased,
With the snow, temperatures decreased

A flying Dutchman did dangle
Andy had the boat to wrangle
Molly had the phone to handle
Eric got his camera angle

Safety demanded a retreat
Seas of ice and skies of cold sleet

The *Nishan Maru* got away
We will get her another day

The Polar winds trapped us in ice
Threatened to lock us in a vice
Dangerous without an ice class
We had to move or be held fast

Bow into that ominous mass
Forcing our way, the only task
Slowly towards open ocean
Advancing in such slow motion

Penguins curious watch us pass
This ice will not hold this ship fast
Heaving growlers before us roll
Such ice could take a lethal toll

House size ice chunks bouncing around
Rolling towards us without sound
Weaving, threading our way through hell
Our thin hull - a vulnerable shell

Breaking through into heavy swell
Heavy surf ringing our brass bell
Between two frozen walls we cruise
Orcas guide us. We cannot lose

Sea Shepherd came through mist and snow
As all around grew wondrous cold
As massive icebergs drifted by
Cobalt blue and pearl white do lie

Probing treacherous deadly rifts
Staring up at chalky white cliffs
The question is not if but when
We can break through this ice and then

Ahead of us upon this course
Killers who suffer no remorse
Life lies ahead for us to save
Keeping gentle giants from the grave

This I know and I know it true
On this planet there are so few
Willing to risk all for a whale
This voyage will be an epic tale

Free Me from the Sea

The midnight sunbeams were dancing over the waves out on the Southern Sea,
Icebergs sparkled like cobalt blue sapphires set in a tiara of profound majesty.

A familiar voice echoed down the years, so haunting in its song,
That voice that had chained me to the sea for far so, very long.
Sweet melodic words that reminded me again that it is love that makes us strong,
Bonded by a curse of gratitude and a promise to right a shameful wrong.

The cold dry air wrapped tightly around me as I stood there on the deck,
And looked in sullen sadness upon our loss, upon that sorry wreck.

Caught unaware we had been rammed and sunk by remorseless cold-blooded whaler men,
In a cowardly attack from the cold-hearted mercenary killers of hot-blooded Leviathan.

I stood upon the deck and listened for that siren's voice that I had once heard so long ago,
And thought of the wearisome battles I have fought for over thirty years or so,

You gave me little choice. In your debt I nailed your colors to our mast.
Your death in the crosshairs of that ship of death, shattered by that harpoon blast.

For decades I have trusted in your wisdom, in your sacred truth to set me free,
Wandering in a martial manner across the stormy seas degree after tedious degree.

My thoughts have traveled in bursts of light across the many turbulent years.
My life has been lived without doubts, without guilt and without normal mortal fears.

All those years of toil, of horror, of frustration, of anger and of strife,
And all the misery, the suffering, the pain, the disappointment and the loss of life.

Into the Pandorian eye of Poseidon I had gazed, searing my soul with a lingering pain.

Into the dark bluish black depths of the sea I stare, searching for truth once again.

Across the shroud of the world's oceans I have fought darkness in your name,
Club and hook, net and harpoon, implements of hatred all the same,
Tearing the wings from the aquatic angels, stripping their bleeding flesh for material gain.

You gave me your promise of protection from death and corruption,
And in return I have fought your quixotic battles without interruption.

And now in this place as the carpet of the sea is swept clean with tears,
And all the whales flee before the horror, their bodies chilled with unknown fears.

I have held your lofty banner, I have held it through victories over humanity's insanity,
I never dropped it once during defeats in the face of human depravity.

Your gift to me has held true, no harm, no freedom lost, for your love did make me strong.
The Southern gales carry your songs into the ear of my heart where they belong,

In closing my eyes, I see your pain, I see your sacrifice, I see my reflection in your eye,
As across the waves my fleet drives relentlessly forward as over the waves we fly.

My senses have been shattered and my soul has crept along the edge of madness,
She is harsh the sea, cold and merciless and a very savage enchantress.

Pursued and pursuing, boarded and boarding, ramming and rammed,

The troubled winds of fury have blown harsh and hot upon my face,
Wondering if ever I will be allowed to retire from the sea with grace.

Knowing that there is only one key to unlock the prison created by that oath I swore,
There can only be one way that I can drop the sword and retire from this endless war

In love is my salvation and it is love that bestows forgiveness,
Allowing me to forsake the sword for the pen, my ships for happiness.

I know longer wish to sail on the deep blue, so much as to gaze into her eyes so blue,
I know longer wish to wrestle and fight with vice, I'd rather embrace her virtue.

Release me from this bond and set me free from my mysterious mistress,
I know that her kiss can break the spell of my aquatic seductive enchantress.

She dances upon the waves of my thoughts, caressing my heart,
To steer a course from the sea I need her tender chart.

I need a bright seductive star to guide me into her warm embrace,
I need so very much to hold her in my arms, to see her pretty face.

For she is my key to the liberation of my soul from the tyranny of the sea,
She will free me, she will cut the bonds from my soul when she finally comes to me.

- Captain Paul Watson June 13th, 2011

The Happy Exile

They detained me Germany in May,
Locked me straight away in their Hessian jail,
The crime of saving the shark and the whale.
They deprived me the right to have my say,
I feared Costa Rica would have their way.
On the eighth day the judge freed me on bail,
House arrest was far better than their jail.
My time in Frankfurt was a pleasant stay,
But politicians were biding their time
The decision had already been made.
Japan was preparing their request,
What I did could surely not be a crime,
Opposing the illegal shark fin trade,
To the crime of compassion, I confess.

Interpol had dismissed Japan's demand,
Costa Rica's demand had been dismissed,
Germany acted outside the Red List,
There would be no fair appeal in Deutschland.
And thus, with no choice but to take a stand,
Departing Germany for the Dutch shore,
Feeling like an escaped prisoner of war.
The situation required a plan,
A small boat to cross the Atlantic Sea,
Onward to cross the Pacific Ocean,
Reaching the far South Pacific Isles.
At long last my flagship had come for me,
I greeted my crew with great emotion,
Japan would have to wait for their files

And so we all prepared for the battle,
The Septics took away our leadership,

I remained a prisoner on my own ship,
The tricolor eagle cast its shadow.
Crossing south of the frigid line at dawn,
We waited for them in the silent fog,
Hourly making entries in the log,
As we tried to address this unjust wrong,
The whalers arrived, our crew drove them west,
Two thousand leagues across the Southern sea,
This year the Ross Sea whales would remain free.
Kept the whalers running, they could not rest,
From the deep dark depths the whales spoke to me.
"This whale sanctuary must remain free."

The fleets came together off the West Ice,
Sun Laurel blocked by the *Steve*, *Bob* and *Sam*.
A road raging *Nisshin* began to ram,
Thrice to the *Bob* and the *Steve* and *Sam* twice.
Against Goliath, the Hammer stood strong,
The towering steel black wall smashed and crashed,

Severed steel wire cables snapped and lashed,
From below the waves came a mournful song.
Doing what we do so the whales may live,
Defending the children of tomorrow,
Opposing the evil forces of greed,
Passion is the gift this brave crew does give,
From our children's future stealing sorrow,
Snatching from Japan what they do not need.

For nine years I've come to this forlorn place,
Year after year confronting the whalers,
Every new year increasing their failures,
Each year across the Southern sea we race,
Each year Sea Shepherd has gotten stronger,

Against a foe of great wealth and power,
But we speak the language of the flower,
Returning each year and staying longer.
They strive to destroy Sea Shepherd and I,
Through politics, media and the court.
The costs are high, the sacrifices great,
No matter the cost we shall always try,
This is a cause we shall never abort,
We must all act now before it's too late.

Thus it has ended for another year,
Cheering as the whalers headed for home,
Escorting killers from the treaty zone.
For far Williamstown, our three ships did steer.
With joy in my heart I saw them depart,
Returning to a warm welcoming crowd,
Received with victorious cheers so loud.
Another voyage marked upon the chart,
I bade them adieu with a happy wave,
There is no safe port anywhere for me,
Save only my mysterious isle.
It is the price that I happily gave,
As a prisoner of freedom on the sea,
Contented to be a happy exile.

- Germany – June 2012

Deceitful Betrayal

Dwelling within a prison without bars,
Afloat on a vast nation, far from land,
From civilization, I have been banned,
Yet still a free man beneath the night stars,
I can but wander here and wander there,
Betrayed by a coward lacking courage,
To the enemy he did encourage,
I was their sought-after prey, he their snare.
Their sly deal was a suspended sentence,
To the Japanese I was thus given,
Framed by politics and betrayed by fear,
With tears, the traitor swore his repentance,
Begging on the bench to be forgiven,
Condemning me to exile last year.

Nine stressful campaigns to the Southern Sea,
Against a foe, influential and rich,
Our long strategy betrayed by a snitch,
In return for an acceptable plea.
This craven Judas holds his head up high,
Strutting and posing for his silly fans,
Posturing with his histrionic plans,
What integrity he had, they did buy,
He cries now that he is misunderstood,
That I am scapegoating him for the blame,
Poor eco-warrior, humble and blameless,
Yes, just a misunderstood Robin Hood,
One died already to further his game,
Yet he remains arrogant and shameless.

His recklessness cost him his trimaran,
He joked and taunted as they ran him down,
It was just luck that the clown did not drown,

His folly found him hauled off to Japan,
And there he claimed I ordered him to board,
He had not a choice he tearfully lied,
None of it at all his fault, he implied
In truth, I had cautioned him not to board.
All on camera for the whole world to see,
Truth be gone once he delivered my head,
I read the false words of his confession,
His foul deceit exiled me to sea,
These whalers won't rest until I am dead,
They may win because of his transgression.

Sparrow on the Deck

T'was a sparrow landed upon our deck,
She drank sweet cool water from Oona's hand.
So far out at sea, such an epic trek,
Her thirst quenched, will she make it back to land?

Each year so many birds blown out to sea,
Desperate to live, so desperate to survive,
So sick at heart for the sight of a tree,
They too have a future for which to strive.

If she could but know and could trust in us,
We could ferry her back to the far shore,
I fear she cannot know, nor in us trust,
For cruel mankind has long since shut that door.

She sits, she watches with a wary eye,
She steps upon an extended finger,
To weak to resist, far to weak to fly,
To regain her strength, she needs to linger.

The sea weeps with the pain of dying birds,
Feathers sink in the murky depths below,
Out of sight, without tears and without words,
This bird touched our heart, and thus our tears did flow.

~ March 30th, 2013

Nowhere Bound

For seven long months I have been at sea.
From Germany in August, I set sail.
As Japan made ready to hunt the whale,
There was no choice but to be free and flee,
I would do no good as a detainee,
I can't defend whales from inside a jail.
Better to weather the Atlantic gale,
Free on the ocean as an escapee,

My mission - stop the killers from Japan,
Across the Pacific to reach my crew,
Then far south to the remote frozen seas,
Joined by two more ships and a trimaran,
Thus began the chase and hullabaloo,
To stop whaling south of sixty degrees.

Chasing them for six thousand miles west,
Intercepting and blocking the slaughter,
Stopping the blood flow into the water,
An excited cry came from the crow's nest.
For nine long years we have followed this quest,
We shall not quit, come hell or high water,

"The Nisshin is coming," cried the spotter,
Her captain rammed us like a man possessed!
All of our ships steadfastly stood their ground,
Until the whaling ships retreated north.
We came, we intervened, we saved the whales,
With the Japanese fleet now homeward bound,

Towards Australia we can now set forth,
Passion and courage never ever fails.

But where to fore is there a place to go,
Condemned as a pirate for saving whales,
So yet once again I must hoist my sails,
My ships may return to the land below,

But upon the vast sea I must lie low,
A fair price for the lives of the great whales,
To see the dark outline of New South Wales,
Those fair shores where I can no longer go.
It would be so nice but not worth the price,
Upon the ocean I must remain free,

So that I may return if the need be,
Once again to the southern seas of ice,
The ocean is not a burden to me,
Life is free and clean on the deep blue sea.

Coming Full Circle

My friends, it is time to re-appear,
The time is upon me. It's clear,
Last year, was not the time, nor the place,
It's time to end this strategic chase.

The ocean has given me her grace,
Also, the chance to prepare my case.
Towards the storm clouds I now shall sail,
Time shall tell if I succeed or fail.

Boreas spreads his cold purple wings,
The strumming wind through the rigging sings,
I've chosen the place where I shall land,
Now is the right time to play my hand.

Upon many shores my crew stands fast,
It's time to challenge Japan at last.
My legal support team is the best,
We are fully prepared for this test.

From Germany to the Southern pole,
Nothing shall dissuade us from our goal.
In defense of marine life we stand,
The world refuses to understand.

I fear the living ocean will die,
Because of humanities dark lie.
Denying the threats of our own greed,
Consuming far, far more than we need.

Because of this I shall pay the price,
And I shall tumble the legal dice,
Into the wild fires I must jump,
For these damn silly charges to trump.

There is a risk in each endeavor,
We know the odds and we know the score.
We shall spit in the eye of our foe,
And before their judgment I will show.

Whatever cost, whatever the price,
The raw strands of truth we need to splice,
To secure all our ships to our cause,
We have no need for praise or applause.

In this quest to defend ocean life,
We expect the sword, the gun, the knife.
I'm prepared for unjust convictions,
By arrogant courts of contradictions,

Henry David Thoreau knew the score,
I know the dangers that wait onshore.
He knew like I know, what must be done.
This struggle must be addressed and won.

I now surrender myself to fate,
To await the judgment of the State.
I see Janus writing on the wall,
I hear the whale songs, I hear them call.

Operation Minke
2005 – 2006

The *Farley Mowat* set off from Aotearoa's shores,
Across the Roaring Forties to remote Commonwealth Bay,
On Christmas day we found the deadly cetacean death star,
And thus began the cold and prolonged Southern Ocean Whale Wars.
Through towering swells our black ship tore through the briny spray,
The *Esperanza's* crew bore witness as we raised the bar.

We crossed the plunging bow of the *Nisshin Maru* with a rope,
The factory ship shuddered and quite quickly sped away,
It took weeks to hunt them down again, no thanks to Greenpeace.
Our ship was much too slow and surprise our only forlorn hope,
The whalers knew we had not come to hang banners and play,
They ran and we forced whaling to temporarily cease.

To South Africa the *Farley* and her crew had to go,
At Japan's request, cowardly Canada took our flag,
Our ship was detained by the South Africans in Cape Town,
No alternative but to make plans somewhat apropos,
Slipping out in the darkness without a national rag,
Across the stormy Indian Ocean, Australia bound.,

Operation Leviathan
2006 – 2007

We needed a faster second ship before returning,
We searched, found, surveyed and purchased the *Westra* in Scotland,
From Europe to Chile's Magellan's Pass to the Ross Sea.
Meeting up with the *Farley*, new tactics we were learning,
We now had two strong ships, one fast, fully equipped and manned,
The new name for the ship? Why *Bob Hunter* it would surely be.

We could now chase and harass the Japanese whaling fleet,
Turning them back from the Ross Sea, chasing them through the fog,
We shut down the spotting ship *Keiko Maru* in the ice,
The *Nisshin Maru* caught fire and Greenpeace did retreat,
Causing us to count many whales saved in this season's log.
One whaler died, but hundreds of whales lived and that was nice.

Both ships lost their flags upon reaching Victoria docks,
Both ships were very quickly reregistered as Dutch yachts,
Greenpeace then called it quits, announcing they would not return,
Whales will not be saved because of banner hanging and talks,
We needed volunteers of passion with a knowledge of knots,
So little time, so much too prepare, to discover, and learn.

Operation Migaloo
2007 – 2008

The great albino humpback inspired our next campaign,
The Aboriginals called him Migaloo, the big white whale,
Steve Irwin would be the one ship for the next voyage South,
We will not abide these magnificent whales being slain,
With this challenge of stopping the whalers we must not fail,
Though we need to all boldly sail into Hell's frozen mouth.

Teri Irwin publicly launched the ship from Melbourne's port,
And Animal Planet sent a film crew for the first time,
Problems with the turbo charger and the crew slowed us down,
Although faced with dire problems we refused to abort,
Repaired we returned to intercept the ongoing crime,
And soon once again the Japanese whaling fleet we found.

Giles Lane and Pottsy boarded the Yushin harpoon ship,
The Australian government responded to gain their release,
Sea Shepherd pursued the whalers out of Australian waters,
Making this, without a doubt the worst Japanese whaling trip,
Greenpeace has been replaced with an aggressive whale police,
Chasing the factory ship, her harpooners and her spotters.

Operation Miyamoto Musashi
2008 – 2009

Taking lessons from the most famous Japanese hero,
This time we engaged the fleet quickly, catching them in the ice,
Yushin harpoon ship down with ice damage and heading home.
Our objective is to get the whale kill down to zero,
Laughing at their useless long-range acoustical device,
Through thick ice and foul weather, the tedious chase does roam.

This season we achieved the blockade with complete success,
Three collisions later the frightened whalers backed away,
Not another whale was slain as we tailed the dark Death Star.
Matching our wits with whalers in a game,
Their bloody decks now bare of carcasses to cut and flay,
We need to dry up the supply to every sushi bar.

This time we chased them for weeks on end across the ocean,
Our long-term objective is to bankrupt the whaling fleet,
We traded rank butter acid stink bombs for stun grenades,
It was a campaign filled with tense action and emotion,
Weathering the deadly ice, the roaring winds and wet sleet,
Took a stray bullet and unleashed the prop fouling brigades.

Operation Waltzing Matilda
2009 – 2010

In August we launched Operation Waltzing Matilda,
In appreciation for Australians and their support,
This time we had a few new surprises for the whalers,
Financed by fund raisers from Fremantle to St. Gilda,
Opposing contempt by the whalers for the Aussie court,
This time three Sea Shepherd ships head south with three crews of sailors.

The flagship *Steve Irwin* out of Fremantle in the West,
From Hobart in the east departs the trimaran *Ady Gil*,
The *Bob Barker* slips out of Mauritius unrevealed,
The *Bob Barker* surprises the whalers from the Northwest,
Struck hard by the *Shonan* the *Ady Gil* crew takes a spill,
Cut in two the *Ady Gil* is lost in the ice field.

In the Kerguelans, the *Bob Barker* and the *Steve Irwin* meet,
The *Steve* returns to port as the *Barker* resumes the chase,
The sorry wreck of the *Ady Gil* elevates the game,
Day after day across the sea the *Bob* chases the fleet,
Repairs are quickly made and the *Irwin* rejoins the race,
Bethune boards the *Shonan* amidst a storm of blame and fame.

Operation No Compromise
2010 - 2011

The trimaran *Gojira* secured for the new campaign,
Bob Barker and *Steve Irwin* prepare the crew in Hobart,
This year we are much better equipped and so much stronger,
The Southern Whale Sanctuary is not Japan's domain.
All three ships head west, spread parallel apart on the chart,
Persistence will allow us to outlast the whalers longer.

We caught the whaling fleet on the first day of the New Year,
The long chase is on for two months through storms, snow, ice and fog,
The *Steve Irwin* searches for lost Norwegian sailors,
The chances of finding them alive were small we did fear,
We found the lifeboat but nothing else as noted in the log,
Bob Barker kept up the pursuit of the fleeing whalers.

The pursuit of the Nisshin went all the way to Chile,
The Chilean Navy made the bold move to intercept,
The whalers surrendered and set a course homeward bound.
The Bob Barker followed through churning seas wild and hilly,
Over the bow the seas broke and across the deck they swept,
At last the key to shutting down these poachers had been found.

Operation Divine Wind
2011 – 2012

The Japanese whaling fleet came down through the Lombok Straits,
We had them until a rogue wave broke the ***Bardot's*** pontoon,
The ***Steve*** rescued the trimaran and returned to the Southern Ocean,
Forest Rescue Simon boarded the ***Shonan*** with his mates,
The small boats attacked and paint balled the ***Yushin's*** harpoon,
Difficult to stop a speeding ship in constant motion.

The chase ran across the top and down into the Ross Sea,
Sea Shepherd crew skirmished with the harpooners through the chase,
The spirit of the Kamikaze we became for the whales,
The storm winds howled like a mortally wounded Banshee,
Humiliated, the whalers returned home in disgrace,
And the ***Bob Barker*** returned in triumph to New South Wales.

The ***Brigitte Bardot*** to Western Australia for repairs,
To Williamstown, Victoria the ***Steve Irwin*** did berth,
Japan attacked us with a small army of lawyers,
Captain Watson's arrest in Germany caught us unawares,
His escape left him an Eco-fugitive upon this Earth,
Yet he returned once again to fight the whale destroyers.

Operation Zero Tolerance
2012 – 2013

After nine years Sea Shepherd stands on the threshold of success,
The Japanese whalers have never left so late from port,
Our interventions have cost them tens of millions of yen,
The whaling industry is in dire financial distress,
Sea Shepherd has been ordered to back off by the U.S. court,
But we shall always be here for the whales again and again.

The *Sam Simon* is the latest addition to the fleet this year,
We tricked the Japanese government, their good ship to sell,
Four Shepherd ships to tackle the whalers this season,
No one is more powerful than a passionate volunteer,
Our crew have the courage to chase the whalers to hell,
And stopping the slaughter of the great whales is the reason.

Where will it go this seemingly never-ending whale war?
What will it take to shut down their bloody whale killing crimes?
Passion, imagination, courage and persistence.
One hundred and twenty crew and ships that number four,
How many more voyages will it take, how many more times?
As long as it takes for we will never cease our resistance.

In the year 2019, Japan ended their illegal operations in the Southern Ocean Whale Sanctuary.

We won and saved the lives of over 6,500 whales.

Made in the USA
Middletown, DE
22 March 2020